A SHORT STORY

LUCKY'S IMAGE

BUSAYO LAWRENCE

I

Misty gray clouds cut through the sky. A dirty blemish of dark spots dotted across its face. The once shimmering light that glowed there was gradually dimming and the last dregs of evening light was trying to find its way behind the graying clouds. It seemed it would rain as the blistered air mixed with the gentle blow of wind that was, in a mild way, swift against the trees.

The grim condition of the weather did nothing to abate the merry moment nearly climaxing in Flat 6, Gemade Estate. The back yard was still packed and children, utterly enraptured by the mood of the day, continued jubilantly in the celebration. For the last time that day Kemi ran around the yard, pushing and shoving the children back towards the yard.

"You'll never get them to listen that way," Ireti had strolled up behind her. Kemi raised herself and wiped a hand across her brow.

"You'd think their parents aren't here, the way these kids are giving me a hell of a time."

"You worry too much about them, that's why. Come, some men have volunteered to watch them. We better get the cake ready before the children lose their fun."

"From what I see, they cannot be distracted from their play. Thanks to the *Balloon man* and the *Muffin man*," Kemi said.

"I wonder where they came from," Ireti asked offhandedly as she put her hand across her friend's shoulder and led her towards the guests.

"From the blues," Kemi was saying.

Ireti looked at her. "From the blues?"

"Yes. They just showed up earlier this afternoon and agreed to do a show for the kids. All for a token. Believe me, those two are life savers," Kemi said.

"Yes, they are. They have been cracking the adults' ribs all day with their banal jokes. Something is off about them though," said Ireti.

Kemi looked thoughtfully at her. "What is off about them?"

"Aunty, nothing. Come, there's someone you've got to meet in the house."

Kemi fidgeted before walking towards the doorway. She looked about and saw some of the kids hurry past the boundary again, past the front yard. She made to go after them. Ireti held her back.

"They're fine. Look, someone's going to fetch them." And truly, a male adult had run towards the children, scolded them, and was leading them to the back of the house. For the umpteenth time before she stepped into the packed house beside Ireti, Kemi wished Tunde was here to witness their daughter, Oluwatoni's birthday celebration.

2

The Balloon man threw up more balloons. The children, overwhelmed with elation, jumped after them. He slipped a hand under the air-filled balloons tied to a stalk on the floor and cut three more loose. A handful number of children had caught the balloons he'd set flying and more had encompassed him, jumping and crying desperately for him to release the bunch in his hand.

He let them run around him, let their cries resonate in his ears, and jutted his hands up, letting them higher and higher. The whole time, a fake smile crossed his face, more for the adults who were watching him, and he never let his eyes slide from the little girl who seemed withdrawn from the crowd; her mates. She was the celebrant.

She was his pick.

He released the first balloon, handed the rope to a small kid, two-year-old perhaps, with three front teeth missing. A ridiculous balance. The boy jumped at the gift and scurried off on his tiny legs, crying, "the balloon man gave me. The balloon man gave me." Actually, his words came out this way, "Bayuu mah gii bee."

A few feet away, Balo 'the muffin man' was playing another prank with the children. He'd repeated this trick five times so far. It was like pulling a rabbit from a hat repeatedly and yet the children were not bored. They kept shouting for more. And were constantly tugging and pulling at his large garment. His face was covered with a white substance, spotted with different colors. His face had been fully painted earlier, but now the painting, which was meant to help mask him, was washing away from perspiration. He heard a sharp click and white light flushed over his face. He looked up. The stupid camera guy had gone and done it to him. He glanced sideways at Tijani 'the balloon man' whose expression told him what trouble to expect if he wasn't careful. He nodded in acquiescence and turned to the children. For another few minutes, he pulled his first trick again the tenth time. The kids shouted. The adults were no longer watching. They obviously were tired of watching the triteness.

Oluwatoni, the birthday celebrant, walked amongst the jumbling children, reached the large bouncing castle and collected the string tied to the balloon from the balloon man. Tijani made sure to wink at her.

"Hey children, want to see what else I've got for you?" Tijani said.

"Yeeeeeeeesssss." The reply echoed around the bouncing castle through the playground. Loud music was crooning from a side where the disc jockey lurked.

"Come on, let's goooo." He would pull the kids away from the adults' watchful eyes. They all seemed distracted but some still had their eyes hovering about, observant, watching him. He heard the click, then the white flash. He spun. The camera guy was smiling as he slipped the digital camera into his back pocket. Tijani's expression tightened, carefully hid by the bulbous clownish nose he wore over the powerfully mascaraed face.

He led the children into the bouncing castle and began playing with them, bouncing up and down and handing stringed balloons to kids who bounced higher. He looked out for the girl again.

She wasn't among them.

Carefully, he bounced towards the edge and looked in Balo's direction. His partner caught the glare and came towards him, leaving his little stand for the children to scatter. He neared the bouncing castle, jumped in beside Tijani and pretended to jump with the kids.

"Where is she?" Tijani asked, unsmiling.

"I saw her with the little boy of that talking mama. I think she got angry because the boy pinned his balloon and ran off."

"Why didn't you follow her?"

"Was I supposed to?"

"You fool! You're supposed to follow her till you get the chance. It's getting dark and I wouldn't want you screwing up my plan 'cos of your nut head."

"Okay I will." Balo made to jump out. Tijani held him.

"Wait. Do you still have the chloroform?"

"Yes, I do. It's right here." He reached into his pocket to bring it out. Tijani whacked him on the head.

"Not here, you dummy. Some adults are watching. You'll give us away. Now find the kid. And get us out of here before this stupid party ends."

"Sure, Tijani. Whatever you say."

"And while you're at it, see if you can knock out that buffoon over there too and get the camera from him. He has our pictures on it."

"Do I have to do all?"

Tijani smacked him again on the head.

"Yes. Not unless you'd want to handle these obnoxious kids who will not let me breath free."

Balo raised both hands in protest.

"Not me. I don't want anything to do with them dumb kids. They made me soil me pant back there. It stinks on me now to high heavens."

"Get off with your task, addle-brain. And remember, two shots and no mistakes."

Balo stepped out of the bouncing castle. Before he had taken three steps towards his stand, the kids were all over him again. Angry, but feigning a smile quickly as a mother emerged from a corner, he began to gesture them towards the castle. He touched his pants as if he'd want to pee and stylishly excused himself.

He walked beside the house towards the low bush by it. He'd seen the kid go there some seconds ago. He looked about. The backyard was teeming with kids, dancing and most running to and from the bouncing castle. The front yard, feet away, had cars parked in front and the adults, a better number of them were in the house. There was no one here to see him.

The little girl was refusing to be placated. She shoved the hand of the boy away. She was crying. The busted balloon lay by her side. She still held on to the string.

The boy was walking.

Balo was walking closer. Darkness was covering the atmosphere. Lights had filled the back of the house and the front. This side was a bit dark. Balo thanked his stars as he got to the kid. He stooped and looked at her, her eyes filled with tears. He couldn't quite see her face now but he could just tell.

"What's wrong, kid?"

"Balloon. Biola bust it."

He put his hand on her shoulder and squeezed gently.

"I'll give you another."

"From the balloon man?" The lilt had returned to her voice.

"From the balloon man." He grabbed the girl from behind and clamped a rag soaked in trichloromethane over her mouth and nose and in an instant the little girl saw nothing but black. He pulled the garment over her, tucked her inside and quickly walked into the low bush.

He'd noticed the path that led to the side of the street, directly close to where the car was parked. He got out at the other end unto the forlorn street, got easily to the car and opened the back seat. He set the girl there and hurried back the same path to the backyard.

Tijani was in the middle of giving away the last set of balloons. He touched his arm and nodded. The other caught on and stoically snuck away from amongst the kids.

Both men snuck easily to their car and didn't pull off their costumes until the car rounded the bend. They drove away.

3

The crowds had gone. The front yard had cleared of cars and the back yard, overly littered, had cleared of the kids. Kemi and Ireti stepped out of the house to the backyard, giggling and then laughing out loud. A bottle of wine hung in the hand of Ireti. She tilted it and filled Kemi's glass. She filled hers. They clinked glasses and started towards the yard. It was empty save for the deflated bouncing castle, dismantled toy cars and houses, empty plastic bottles and Biola kicking cans around into a makeshift goalpost of a toy donkey and zebra few distances apart.

The mothers walked close to him. Kemi looked about, surprise filling her face.

"Biola, where's Toni?"

The boy kicked two more cans through the goalpost, raised both hands in triumph and looked at the women. He shrugged his shoulders.

"What'd you mean you don't know? Weren't you two together?" Ireti asked, leaning forward towards him.

The boy shrugged his shoulders again. Ireti and Kemi began looking about. After ten fruitless minutes of searching about the house for the little girl, Kemi was frenetic as she hurriedly wandered about the compound, about the house, up the stairs and down again. All the while Ireti doing the same. Both saw Femi's car pull up in front of the house. They hurried towards the door, towards Femi. Kemi ducked into the car, briefly ignoring Femi's greeting.

"And good evening to me, too," Femi said. "What's the frenzy about? You don't expect me to buy chicken and chips for adults like you two."

"We thought you drove out with Oluwatoni, sweetheart."

"Oluwatoni?"

"Yes."

"What's happened to her? I went to get her the teddy bear I promised her. I didn't want the little girl thinking her uncle's a liar."

"We can't find her, Femi. We've looked for her everywhere. I think...I think she's missing."

Kemi had ducked out of the car and had heard the statement.

"No. No. My baby could never be missing. We've not looked around enough yet." She was visibly shaking. Her face wet with tears.

"I've you checked the house?" Femi asked.

"Thoroughly," replied Ireti.

"We'll looked around the street and asked around. She could be anywhere around. Perhaps, she followed a friend home. Remember Chimezie's son did the same thing at his birthday party last week. You never can tell with these kids. Where's Biola?"

"At the back."

"Keep him in the house. Or better still I'll ask around. Both of you can go in and search again. Have you called Tunde yet?"

"He hasn't called all day," Kemi said.

"Nuts, Tunde," Femi jammed his hand onto his palm. "Call him...and get his reaction before you call the police."

"The police...my baby...my baby." Kemi was withdrawing, tears pouring down her face in mild torrents.

"It's going to be alright, Lucky. We'll find her," Turning to his wife, "Ireti, search the house, and no matter what happens, stay with her. I'll be back." And he hurried off.

The women hurried into the house. Kemi grabbed her phone immediately and dialled Tunde's number. He picked on the third ring.

"Hey hon, I'm sorry I couldn't call you. I had a rather busy day..."

"Toni is missing."

"I'll be back late tonight but kiss my girl for me."

"TONI IS MISSING, Tunde!"

"What!...what...how, where?"

"We can't find her around the house. Biola hasn't seen her. Femi has gone to ask around. I'm going with him now. I just thought to call you."

"You call the police immediately. And you'd better find my child before I return. You careless..."

"Don't dare put this on me Tunde. Your back is broken now and you're at the blame game all over again. Pray I find my child. Just pray I find her. Please God, let me find my baby." She hung up before he could say anything more.

She tossed the phone aside and made to rush outside the house to join Femi. The door opened instantly. Femi stood by it, panting and wearing a worried look.

"No one has seen her. I asked all the neighbours and even had some of them ask their children and look around their apartments. No one has seen her. We better call the police. I'll do that." He hurried past Kemi and got to the phone. The Maryland Police Division answered and Femi made the report. The women were gathered around him. He hung up and looked at Kemi.

"They'll be here shortly."

"My baby. My precious baby." Kemi sloped to the floor and began crying. Seconds later she arose again and scurried out of the house. Femi and Ireti were hurrying and calling after her.

"I have to find my baby." She began screaming along the street. Two neighbors, an old man and woman, got out of their house and stopped to look at flustered Kemi. Kemi neared them and stood below the terrace.

"Have you seen Oluwatoni, Mr. Igwe?"

The older folks looked at each other and then back at Kemi. They shook their heads.

"My baby is missing." She burst into tears again. Femi and Ireti took her and led her away.

When she was back in the house, they made her sit. Ireti held her hand and placated her. A rasp knock came on the door. Femi hurried to get it. Kemi was on her feet to go with him. The door opened and two police officers walked in.

"Good evening. We got your call." One of the men said.

"Yes sir. Do come in." Femi led them in and offered them a seat.

"I'm detective Richard and my partner's name is Detective Uche. Do you want to tell us what actually happened here?"

Kemi was crying profusely. She spoke up amid tears. "My baby's missing."

"How old is she?" asked one of the detectives.

"She turned **four** today," Kemi replied.

"How long has she been missing?"

"We don't know. We just found out say 2 hours ago." Femi spoke up.

The detectives looked at each other.

"What happened here?" asked Detective Richard.

"Today is her birthday. We had a celebration for her..."

"And then she suddenly went missing afterwards?"

"We were all in the house. The children were at the back of the house. Safe as we last observed. We can't say what happened afterwards. Cars drove away and the kids and their parents all left. We have called all the parents that were here to ask. My husband has had to visit their houses, too." Ireti said.

"We'll need a list of all the parents that were here today."

"I'll write that," Ireti said.

"Good. Did you notice any strange occurrence, you know, a stranger coming in or someone you know who may be slightly off-looking to you?"

"No..." Kemi started to say.

"Yes," Ireti cut in. "Some two funny-looking men were here: the balloon man and the muffin man. They showed up this afternoon and gave a show to the kids. They agreed to collect a token but I doubt that they waited to collect it." She looked at Kemi, who shook her head. No.

"You don't know anything about these men?" The detective directed the question at Kemi.

"No, I don't."

Richard gestured to his partner. They both arose.

"We'll look around if you don't mind. And we'll need light."

Ireti arose and fetched them a lamp. The detectives walked out of the house. Femi followed behind them. They didn't object.

A car had arrived in front of the house. Kemi started to her feet just as the door opened.

"Where's she? Where's my daughter? Where's Toni?" Tunde rapped off as soon as he stepped through the door.

Femi had just come in through the back door. "Cool it, Tunde. You haven't been available all day. So, don't make things worse for your wife."

"If she'd watch over her well, she wouldn't be missing."

"Watch your mouth, Tunde." Kemi stood to her feet. "You're the uncaring father who got so lost in your job and your lowlife girlfriends you could not be here to give your child the protection she needed. You have to help me find my daughter. Otherwise, on this, we're done!"

Tunde cast his suit aside, pulled his tie and undid two buttons. He swerved into the room and neared Kemi, unmoved by her tear-filled face. Just then the back door opened. The two detectives walked in.

"Who is this?" Detective Richard asked.

"I'm her father. Who are you?" Tunde advanced towards them.

"Detective Richard. Here's detective Uche." He thrust out his hand for a handshake. Tunde ignored it.

"What have you found?"

"These." Richard extended his hand. The others swarm around him. In his grasp was a Barbie doll and a small comb.

"That's Oluwatoni's. That's my baby's." Kemi shoved forward and grabbed the doll.

"Then whose is this?" Richard asked, showing her the comb.

"Where'd you find this?"

"We found them together beside the house. And there were footprints along the small bush behind your house."

"Yes. It was supposed to be cleared before today. I gave her money for it." Tunde said, looking cruelly at Kemi who didn't bother to meet his gaze but was crying over the doll in her hand.

"If this isn't hers, then whose is it?"

Just then the back door opened. Biola walked in.

"I thought I told you to bring him in," Femi started at Ireti.

"Your son?" Richard asked.

"Yes." Femi replied. "He and Oluwatoni are very good friends."

"Then he may know who owns this. Come boy."

"Come here Biola." Femi called.

The boy walked forward and stopped in the middle of the room. Richard held his palm open and showed the comb to the boy.

"Hey, Biola, do you know who owns this?" Richard asked.

The boy gave no response.

"If you'll let me detective," Femi said.

"Certainly." The detective stepped aside.

"Biola, who is owner of this comb? Is it for Toni?" The boy shook his head, no. "Who owns it then?"

His lips moved.

"Eh," the detective leaned closer.

Femi tilted his ears close to him. He was mumbling again. He heard. Femi mouthed it. "The muffin man."

"Were you with Toni?"

"No. She left. I left too. Then she left with him."

"With who?" Kemi's edgy voice carried off in the atmosphere.

"The bayuuum man." The boy pantomimed a flying balloon, spontaneously jumped up and down and began running around.

"The balloon man. The...balloon man." Kemi felt her feet turn cold. Hot chills slapped her spine and fingered them in quick torrents. The doll in her hand slipped to the floor. She was losing consciousness.

"My baby...my poor baby." Ireti held her.

"Do you have a photo perhaps? Can you describe this man."

"Men. Two. They were two. I knew those lots were up to no good. I just should have trusted my instinct." Ireti said.

"Photos. Description."

"I can't describe them. They were decked in clownish garments. Their faces were hidden. I can't say I had a close look at them."

"Matthew took pictures today. He must have taken a picture of them. We could get their snapshots from his camera," Ireti said.

"Where's this Matthew?"

"He lives down the street."

They got Matthew. The teenager produced his digital camera. The display screen was broken so that pictures could not be viewed. The detectives drove Kemi and Tunde to the station.

4

"How are they doing?" Detective Richard asked the station's secretary.

"They are still having it off with each other in there. It's a good thing the door is sound-proof. They're ready to kill themselves in there. Remind me to never get married," The fat lady said.

"Haba! For what? More seriously, I need you to blow up this picture for me if you will. And give me a print as soon as possible. Think you can do it?"

"No sweat, detective," the lady said.

Detective Richard returned to his office. Kemi and Tunde were still arguing.

"It's your fault this is happening, Kemi. Why not just admit it."

"If you'll just cool it and swallow your botched up ego for once, Tunde. I'm sick and tired of your blame game. I'm done enduring this little piece of nonsense you call marriage. You'll get to meet my lawyer after this. I have the papers for you. This sick-stupid thing is done."

"You just pray I find my daughter, Kemi. Just pray so. Or I'll have your..."

Detective Richard interrupted with a cough.

"The picture is being printed. Now if you'll just fill the statement in front of you, we can get going with that."

The two quieted and looked at the papers in front of them. They both hesitated before pulling it closer and began to fill.

5

Balo nursed the wound on his nose again. He was mindful of Tijani's incessant glare, had gotten used to it and had decidedly been ignoring it.

"I pulled that nonsense thing too tight on me nose. Now he peeled me."

"You fool. I told you to wear tissue over it before you put it on." Tijani replied, not taking his eyes off the road. A car swerved in his direction, cut over to his side and moved between his car and another in front. Tijani cursed and thumped the steering wheel concurrently.

"You made it."

"What?" Tijani asked, not quite hearing him.

"You made the thing. Why'd you made it too tight? To punish me for sleeping in your bed last night?"

Tijani spun at him. "You slept in my bed? You slept in my bed you little...punk." He whacked him on the head.

"You wasn't at home. And I felt lonely in me little room."

"Weren't, dunce. You weren't at home."

"Whareva. You..."

"Whatever. You have to learn to speak well. Otherwise, you'll keep giving us away."

"I been doing well ever since. You not been commending me like you use to. You spoilt my motivation there."

"Okay, you are doing good you, little imbecile. Satisfied?"

"What does *beembesal* mean?"

"It means you're good. Now shut it and let me get down to driving this thing out of here. Nuts! The sodding traffic is jamming up now."

The car slowed and began moving slowly behind the long row of cars. Except for the lights spilling from the street lights unto a part of the dashboard, there was darkness in the car. Tijani looked at the back seat. The kid was still sprawled there. He mentally counted the amount he'd demand from the parents. He'd changed it so many times in his mind along the way.

"How many doses did you give her?" Tijani asked.

Balo was thrusting his fingers through his nose, bringing each out and cleaning them against his rumpled shirt. "One."

The smack landed on his head before he could look at Tijani's face. "You fool. I thought I said..."

"Two. It's two. And quit knocking me on the head. You making me soil me fingers."

"You fool, you are sure it's two?"

"On my mama's grave."

Tijani smacked him again. "Ouch. Stop eet."

"Your mother hasno grave. She was cremated. Remember?"

"Okay. I almost forgot. Of course, she was. So, on my mother's ashes. That good enough?"

"Shoot yourself, imbecile."

"*Beembisal* don't mean good then."

"Just shut it, will you."

For the next few minutes Tijani concentrated on the drive. The traffic was slowly moving. There was a sudden stop. No car moving. Tijani slapped the steering wheel again, cursed louder than before.

A car had broken down ahead.

The honks of cars blared in the night. Light spilled across the road, catching a lad who had just reached into the car in front of Tijani's and had grabbed the driver's purse. The woman got down and began shouting as the lad made away with the purse.

Tijani got down also and walked towards the woman to get her car off the road. Balo remained in the car, busily running all his fingers through his nose.

The girl started awake when the noise got louder. Her eyes were still trying to adjust to the darkness in the car as she mumbled, "Mummy, mummy." Her voice, truncated and tired, did not reach Balo who had plugged an earpiece into his ears, bobbing as the rock song blared from the small music player in his pocket.

Oluwatoni arose slowly. Her head ached lightly. She looked at the man in the front seat. He didn't look familiar. She clasped her hand and set them on her lap. She felt her stomach tightening. She was slightly hungry.

"Mummy...Mummy." She began sobbing. She wanted to touch the man in the front and tell him to take her home. Her head was clearing. In her mind's eye, she saw the man then. She'd seen him today. He'd offered her a gift. He'd promised to give her...balloon. The balloon man. The muffin man. He'd put a cloth over her nose and it had peppered her. She'd slept then. On the floor? May be.

The man was getting down. The side door opened and closed again. The man was gone. He hadn't heard her cry. And he was leaving her. She would follow him. No, she won't. Mummy said not to follow strangers. The man could be boogie man. He could carry her to his castle and never let her see Mummy again. Then she would sleep for a hundred years and someone, may be Biola, would then come for her.

She didn't want to go to that castle. The car was empty now except for her. She looked at the side door. Mummy had taught her to open the door. "Raise this clip and push." She raised the clip and pushed the door. It opened easily and she stepped out.

The cold air hit her face. She wrapped her hand around herself and started away from the car. A boy selling sausage roll came towards her. Oluwatoni moved to the car. The boy walked past, carrying two opened cartons and hurrying towards a car.

She looked about her. There were cars around. So many. Like Cars cartoon. If she could find a smaller one, she would drive out of here. She remembered her toy car. She would sit in it while Biola would push. They always get somewhere together that way, driving across the front lawn to the backyard. Biola had spoilt the wheel two days ago. Daddy had promised to buy a real car for her. When she was older. Like Mummy.

She walked past a car and glimpsed the passenger's side. A child was looking at her from there. He was eating sausage roll and had just cast the wrapper on the floor.

Mummy would never like that. She'd made her spell those words repeatedly that had now stuck with her.

U-n-p-a-t-r-i-o-t-i-c N-i-g-e-r-i-a-n.

Mummy said you were an unpatriotic Nigerian if you threw things on the floor. Then she would've spanked her. She ignored the boy as he rolled his tongue at her. She walked away, past the cars, past the road, unto the sidewalk where she began looking at the tall buildings and too many people walking up and down this area. As pangs began to finger her stomach, Oluwatoni looked slowly about.

A tinge of familiarity was biting at her heart.

6

The door opened. The fat lady walked in.

"You wouldn't believe what I have, sir," she started.

"What do you have?" Detective Richard was alert. Kemi and Tunde turned, their gaze fixed on the lady. She ran a hand over the A4 size manilla envelop in her hand, opened it and brought out some files.

"I did a blow up of the pictures you chose. The men were dressed as clowns. Nice cover up. They faces were masked."

"That I know..." The detective interjected.

"But another of the what now-yes, muffin man-came and I did that soon. I got a clear picture then. The mask was gone. Thanks to perspiration."

"Get to point, Helen."

"Patience, detective. I thought I recognised the person in the picture and so I looked up our database. Lo, the clown has some issues with us in the past. Two, as I saw. Here, see for yourself."

She set the files on the table. Detective Richard turned it towards him and looked it over. Kemi and Tunde were all over him, both gawking at the enlarged picture of a man garbed in a clown garment and disguise but whose face had been duly captured. The face matched the other face on the next photo beside the new one. A profile of the clown was beside it also.

"Splendid! I know this rogue. And he doesn't work alone. You said they were two, right?" He looked up at Kemi.

"Yes."

"Then its Tijani and Balo. Foolish rogues. I told them to never cross my path again. Now they've messed up big time. Don't worry Mr. and Mrs. Kolawole. I know just where to find these men."

"We'll come with you," started Tunde.

"No, you won't. You'll go home and wait for me. I'll just be out for, say, an hour. Those two are going to be in our custody."

"And my daughter," Kemi said.

"And your daughter." Detective Richard looked at Helen who was standing by the door, obviously waiting for credit for the discovery she'd made. "Good work, Helen."

"Thanks detective, anything I can do to help..."

"Reach Uche for me. Tell him we're going out. This ought to be easy."

Helen walked out, got to her desk and reached Uche. The detective showed up soon and both detectives went away in the patrol car. The Kolawoles defiantly waited at the station.

7

Oluwatoni recognized this place now. Mummy had brought her here when she'd come to pick a dress for her for Biola's birthday. Here they'd picked beautiful toys for Biola. Toys Biola had discarded, complaining her mummy hadn't bought her fine toys like hers. She'd promised to share hers with him then.

Biola was a good friend. But he could be naughty sometimes. Oluwatoni thought. He'd found her when she had slept off under her mother's bed and everyone in the house was looking for her. Mummy had called Biola her hero then. The name had stuck and she'd called him, "my *yeeero*" occasionally.

Only he was not around to find her now. She was hungry. She'd been walking around the sidewalk the whole time, gawking endlessly at the rows of beautiful shops.

A car had nearly splashed water on her. She'd quickly sidestepped, bumping into an old man who bared his dark charred teeth at her. Oluwatoni had quickly hurried away. The man had looked too scary.

She'd stopped in front of the toy shop where Mummy had taken her to buy Biola's toy. There was so much light there. And toys were looking at her from their cage. She'd asked mummy why they always have to be in that cage. She could see them, the cage colour like water, but she could not touch them from here. Mummy had said it was to protect them. From running away? She couldn't remember what mummy had said thereafter.

Perhaps she could go in and sit. And Mummy would come in and find her. Mummy had talked friendly with the fat woman who'd attended to them. No. The fat woman was a stranger, too.

She looked ahead. There was a stand ahead and the man was selling ice cream and cakes. Oluwatoni wished she had money now. How much would those sell for? She'd known to identify the currency notes. Blue and crispy meant fifty naira. Green and crispy with the picture of a soldier man with full hair meant twenty naira. And ten naira was red with the picture of a smiling teacher man who had glasses on his face like grandma's. She was hungry. Mummy said too much hunger wasn't good for the body.

She remembered.

She poked her hand into her pocket and felt the money. It was still there. Aunty Ireti had given her earlier today. She could identify what amount it was. Green and dirty with two and two zeros. She approached the man. She didn't want to go alone. The man may cheat her or take her away. She saw a woman standing close to the place and her child beside her. Oluwatoni got close and stretched out the money.

"Which one do you want, little angel?" The man said. His teeth were very dirty and two front teeth were lost. Oluwatoni pointed at the ice cream and the cake.

"One cone coming right up for you. Your Mummy will soon be leaving." He said, looking up at the woman who was starting to move. Oluwatoni leaned closer.

Oluwatoni wanted to say the woman wasn't her mummy but she kept quiet. She hadn't lied that way, had she?

Mummy always make her call Aunty Ireti "Mummy". Older women were Mummy. And so, she hadn't lied.

She collected the cone and the cake, waited to see if she'd receive a change. She did. The man handed her one note to her. She looked at the picture of the old man in cap. A figure 5 and 0 was on it. Yes, 50 naira.

She walked away, sipping her ice cream and biting her cake, the cold night pinching her skin. She stepped down from the sidewalk, looked to the right and to the left and to the right again before crossing the street. She got to the next sidewalk. Her legs were getting tired. She saw the bench behind the sidewalk by the electric pole. She walked towards it and sat upon. She watched as a little girl ran to catch up with her mother who was walking ahead of her. The girl was crying.

Oluwatoni felt she'd cry, too. No. She won't. Biola said only little girls cry. And she wasn't a little girl. This other girl was. And that's why she's got her cloth dirty and she's tugging at her mummy's cloth. Oluwatoni could not hold back the hurt any longer.

"Mummy where are you?" She said and bit into the last bit of ice cream.

As the wind blew cold breeze again, whispering through her hair and caressing her face, she closed her eyes a brief moment, oblivious to the man lurking and watching her in the lone stall behind. The man who'd been following her all along.

8

Detective Richard found the bar easily. He pushed the bat-winged door open and made a beeline to the bar. The bartender, a sturdy man with a hard feature, cleanly chiseled face and curt chin that was fully bearded, was cleaning a glass. He set the glass down as the detective neared the bar, nearing him. Detective Richard left out pleasantries, clasped a hand around the clean glass and peered into the man's eyes. It flickered shut and opened again, like it was trying to figure who this was.

"Cut the nonsense, Ganduje and tell me where they are at."

"Who are 'they'?" Ganduje asked, his voice husky. Detective Richard did not miss the tremor in that voice. One mistake from this man and he could hurl him back to jail where he'd personally put him in the first place. By sheer luck, the bartender had missed serving five years in the penitentiary.

"I have strings I could pull and you'll find yourself behind the metals again. I could fix you up with some wrongs I'll make certain to dig up myself. This time I'll make you rot in there. No bail."

Ganduje flinched, fretting. "I don't know what you talking about. I'm clean." His voice was shaking, his hands trembling as the napkin slipped from his grasp.

"Of course, you are. That's why you're here. But you have friends who aren't."

"Friends?"

"Yes, friends. I need to find Balo. You know, the imbecile that got you into the trouble that first landed your butt behind bars."

"Balo? I've been done with Balo a long time. He rarely comes here now."

"Does he? Info tells me he was here two days ago. I need to locate him and Tijani. Or I'm goin' to have to pick you instead. You decide what's the call."

"What gives, mehn? I haven't done nothing."

"Quit **dogshitting** me and tell me where to find them. Or do you need me to call the next dog?" He gestured at Uche who was standing by the entrance now, nudging something under his shirt. A gun? A cuff? Ganduje couldn't tell. Didn't want to tell.

Detective Richard was looking straight at him. His brow was chilled in spite of the fans cooling the room. He knew why they called this detective Richard the Morgue man. He'd done enough cleaning the street of most of his fans. Stern and cruel with some mind-bugging intelligence.

"They are at Celestial Street. 3rd house to your left. Room six. First floor."

"Thanks, Ganduje." Silence. Detective Richard turned the cup in his hand. "Care to fill my cup?"

The burly man eyed him. Richard took his leave.

9

Oluwatoni could see the boogie man in her dream. He was drawing closer and was ready take her away. Take her away from Mummy and Biola and Daddy and Aunty Ireti, No, Mummy, and everyone. The place he would take her would be dark and scary. And there would be slimes and earthworms.

Earthworms!

That made her stomach. She hated the slimy thing. And the boogie man was slimy like them. So, she won't let him take her.

She forced herself awake.

The ice cream cup and cake wrapper had slipped from her grasp. She flickered her eyes open and rested against the bench. Cars were running past and the street lights bounced on her face. She saw a shadow beside her, like hands raised to catch her.

The boogie man!

She jumped down from the bench, hurried forward and pivoted. A man was standing there, had probably been standing behind her, and was going to take her. He had deliberately hidden himself from the light.

The boogie man.

The boogie man. He had come from the grave. The boogie man. Oluwatoni knew her heart was beating fast. She was afraid. That was why she couldn't control her heart beat. Mummy said to put your hand on your chest when you're afraid and wait and count to ten. She was going to do that when the man began walking forward.

Oluwatoni didn't know what to do. The sidewalk was thinly used. Few people were passing. She saw a woman coming down the sidewalk and holding a large bag, one that looked the type mummy had in her wardrobe. She quickly approached the woman and tucked her hand into hers.

The woman looked down at her a moment and smiled.

"Little girl, what're you doing here?" The woman's hand was wet against her palm. Oluwatoni didn't like it so she quickly released her hand. The boogie man was backing away slowly.

"Mummy said call."

"Call? Your mother left you?"

"No. She's there." Oluwatoni pointed forward. The woman looked forward. A woman was standing by a kiosk, leaning every now and then over two kids. The lady started to walk, holding Oluwatoni. They crossed to another sidewalk and the woman would have taken her to the other woman. Oluwatoni stopped abruptly.

"What, little girl? I'll take you to mummy."

"I go myself." She remained there, her hands folded across her chest.

"Okay then. Bye."

Oluwatoni waved to her. The woman waited, looked at her and then back at the woman. Oluwatoni decidedly waved at the other woman. The kids waved back. This woman smiled then and walked away.

When Oluwatoni saw she was gone, she started into the big street before her. People were plenty here and she couldn't see the boogie man anymore. A brief thought passed through her mind.

What had she told the woman earlier? Yes. Mummy said call. She had money in her pocket. She knew her Mummy's phone number. Mummy had made her recite it and memorise it. And she'd seen Mummy walk to a shed like the one ahead and call Daddy.

"Mummy, why didn't you use the phone at home?"

"It's not calling out for now dear. I'll call Daddy here and pay. Then we'll return to the house."

Oluwatoni hurried to the stand and stood before the lady sitting on a yellow chair under a yellow umbrella.

"Call."

The lady looked at her, searched her face for whatever purpose and then dug into her bag. She handed the phone to Oluwatoni then quickly retrieved it.

"Where's your money?"

Oluwatoni brought the blue note.

"Call the number."

Oluwatoni touched the side of her temple, closed her eyes and pictured the scrawl she'd made beneath the bar in the kitchen. She read out the number so easily. She waited. After some seconds, the lady gave her the phone. She put it to her ear. It was beating in her ear.

Ringing.

10

Detective Richard let his eyes slide over to the couple.

"I'm convinced they're telling the truth. They missed the kid somewhere."

It had been easy to find the two rogues. He and Uche had found the house and quickly identified the room. They hadn't needed to break in or knock. The door was open and both men were quarelling heatedly at the time. Richard and Uche had simply registered their conversation, noted it was blame game over some lost kid, and had been able to put one and two together.

"You have to press them officer. They have to know where my child is," Tunde said.

"I'm so sure. They're bunch of imbecilic thieves. Too dull not to tell the truth in the face of jail threat. Not that they would ever miss it this time."

"My baby. Where have they left her? Did they say?" Kemi said, sobbing.

"Somewhere around Dopemu Roundabout. She must have slipped out of the car while they were quarreling with some lady whose car was blocking theirs."

"What do we do now?"

"We begin to search. But might I ask, does your daughter know anything that could be helpful. You know, friends who live close, phone number, anything that could help."

"No." Tunde said.

"Yes," Kemi chipped in. "I made her memorise my phone number. Oh God, I left my phone at home."

"Do you think she'd be smart enough to call if there was trouble?"

"She called from school twice when the school bus left her behind. She'd be smart enough to call. But I doubt...I doubt..." Kemi couldn't bring herself to say it.

"Relax Mrs. Kolawole. Maybe you should get home and find out if she's called.

"Femi and Ireti are still there. We can reach them from here," Tunde said.

"Good. Let's do that."

II

Femi and Ireti had just finished making a short prayer for Oluwatoni, Kemi and Tunde when Ireti's phone vibrated on the chair. Ireti reached for it and punched the green button.

"Yes."

It was Kemi. They'd found the kidnappers but Oluwatoni was not with them. She was missing. She was asking if Oluwatoni perhaps had called.

"No, she hasn't," Ireti replied, dejection lacing her voice.

She talked for a while and the phone cut. Femi was looking at her. She narrated what she'd heard. Femi splayed his hands by his side when he heard Oluwatoni was missing.

"They have to find her," Femi said.

"They will. I pray they do," Ireti said.

Biola walked into the room. Ireti looked at him. His cloth was soiled with ketchup which he had found in the kitchen.

Ireti had thought she heard Biola talking to someone on the phone right in the kitchen. The boy stopped in the sitting room, picked up the ball he had left there and started to run away again.

"Whose phone were you with, Biola?"

"Mrs. Kolawole's phone."

"I thought I warned you never to pick someone's call without their knowledge. Who was that on the phone?"

The boy paused for a while.

"Oluwatoni."

He said as he raced into the kitchen.

12

Kemi was dejected. Her heart was racing too fast like it would pop out of her chest. Her hands were tightening around the seat. The kidnappers had been found. But Oluwatoni was missing. They took her daughter. Now they lost her. And Oluwatoni hadn't called. She was walking the streets alone. How long before she was taken again? By a stranger. A killer.

"Now that side is botched. We'll have to figure something out," the detective was saying.

"If Oluwatoni hasn't called, does it imply anything? I can't think of it, detective. My daughter may be somewhere, with some stranger."

"Let's just hope something comes up. I might have to see those buffoons again. Perhaps there's something they left out."

Detective Richard stood to leave. Kemi's phone rang immediately. She picked it. Then gave a low scream. The detective stopped by the door. Kemi hung up, looked into Tunde's eyes and back at the detective.

"That was Ireti. Oluwatoni called."

13

Oluwatoni reached the end of the large street and started again in the right direction. She'd seen this place before. Mummy had brought her here. What had happened then? Yes. She'd asked so many questions and Mummy had given her answers to them. Why was this place big? What was the name? Will Father Christmas ever come here?

Then they walked past a big house. Mummy had called it a church. There was the crucifix of Jesus in front of it. The crucifix was in small house and she had gone there, sat in it and had looked at Jesus's face. His two fingers bunched together spread out over her. There had been no tears on His face like she'd learned.

Why wasn't He crying?

She'd stayed there, slept, and then mummy had found her. Mummy was almost crying then. Why? Mummy hadn't responded. She'd only held her close and pushed her head onto her chest.

Oluwatoni had memorised the name of the place. She'd seen it, stared at it and had asked Mummy to pronounce it for her.

It spelt C-h-r-i-s-t C-a-t-h-o-l-i-c C-h-u-r-c-h.

She wanted to go there again, to see that Jesus who didn't cry. There were always too many people around there but she would find a space for herself. She needed to ask someone first.

A police man was standing by the roadside. He was holding a baton and gesturing at a dirty boy to leave the side of road. Oluwatoni walked towards him and pulled the side of his trouser. The man looked down at her.

"Christ Catholic Church."

"CCC daughter? You have to walk straight down. It's down by the left. It should be easy to see. What, you're not with your mama?"

"She's there," Oluwatoni pointed at a random place. The police got distracted when a woman screamed thief. The dirty boy was running away. The police gave a chase.

Oluwatoni started to walk towards the area. She would see Jesus there. She felt her heart lighten.

She was happy.

14

Detective Richard hung up. The operator had given the location.

"It's somewhere around Agege. That's her last location."

"We have to go," Kemi said.

"I'll go with you," Ireti said.

"Our officers will begin to comb the place."

"I will go with you," Kemi said again.

"No."

"I know the place well. We have been there together so many times."

"Suit yourself."

"We'll stay back and wait in case something else comes up," Femi said and looked at Ireti.

"Yes. That's better."

Kemi got a large picture of Oluwatoni. The detective drove back to the station to round up his men. Tunde sloped into the car. Kemi fell beside him. They drove on.

Tunde's phone rang again. The tenth time that night.

"Pick your calls Tunde. It could be your partners. Don't forget to tell them they're disturbing my peace."

"Cut it off, Lucky."

"I'm not cutting it off, Tunde. You could've been there to save her. You could've. You could've..." She began to cry again. "My baby. My poor baby."

She raised her head. "What did you say?"

Tunde had muttered under his breath.

"I said where did we begin to fall apart?"

There was quietness in the car. Kemi didn't want to think about the question. But it was gnawing at her heart. Why had they begun to fall apart?

When Tunde had begun keeping late nights. When he'd stopped listening or paying attention. When he'd stopped caring for her and Oluwatoni and he'd submerged himself in work. When he'd began giving excuses on how he had to take good care of his family.

Yes, they began to fall apart when he began to love his work than his family.

But was that true?

She fiddled with the thought.

Tunde had loved her, shown her he cared too much. She'd began complaining when it seemed the care was dwindling. He'd attempted to change. It had seemed forced at the time.

Or was it?

The man had been trying his best. But she'd began seeing something else. Tunde wasn't like he used to be. Work or no work she still deserved the care he showered on her before they were ever married. Before Oluwatoni was born.

Oluwatoni.

Had she taken Tunde from him? Her daughter competing with her? No. She was wrong. She saw it. She was beginning to see this in another light. She was wrong. She had been. Had she pushed Tunde away? He's so close yet he seemed so distant.

Oluwatoni, be safe. Please be safe for mummy, sweetheart.

"Somewhere we stopped paying attention to what's most important to us," Kemi said.

Tunde looked at her.

"And what's most important to us?"

"What do you think it is?"

Tunde looked at her again. "I don't know. I haven't figured it out yet," he replied.

"We both haven't," Kemi added.

Silence hung between them. Her heart was quietening. Somewhere within Kemi, there was going to be a way around this. Hadn't the divorce lawyer said so? "There's always a way around everything." She didn't know she had said it out loud.

"A way around everything? Have I not heard that before?"

"She told me," Kemi said.

"Who told you?"

Kemi looked outside the window. The road was slightly busy. They were nearing Agege now. Darkness had covered the atmosphere. Cars were speeding by. Was her daughter in one of them?

"Who told you," Tunde asked again.

"You don't want to know."

Minutes later, they stopped at a corner in Agege. They both alighted. Kemi quickly brought out the picture and ran across the road. Oluwatoni had loved the Toy Shop. If she had been here, she would come close to it or even might have entered it.

No, the fat woman said, she hadn't seen the little girl. Tunde was right behind her as she raced out again. They began asking people around. They'd combed so many areas within the space of thirty minutes.

The night was cold. Chilly air was biting into their skins. Tunde pulled her close as they neared the car, ready to move to another location. His phone had been ringing the whole time.

"Pick it, Tunde. I insist," Kemi said calmly.

"It's my boss, Lucky. He could be calling for another..."

"Go ahead. Just do it."

"Okay." He picked the call. They were sitting in the car. Kemi was still looking around for her daughter.

"Yes. No problem." Tunde ended the call. He was downcast.

"What happened?" Kemi asked.

"He cut me off. I worked nights and days for three months for the deal and he cut me off."

"Your boss?"

"Yes."

"What, because you miss the meeting?"

He looked at her. "Would I rather be at some stupid meeting while my daughter is missing?"

Silence.

"No, you won't. You won't, Tunde." She slipped her hand over his. He closed his over hers and for a while their eyes locked. This was it. This was what she'd been missing. He loved her dearly and yet she'd been too blind to see it. Coincidentally, Tunde was thinking the same.

"Come, let's go find our daughter. She has to be here so somewhere. Jesus baby she is."

"Jesus baby! Yes, that's what I've been trying to figure out." Kemi said.

"What is it, hon?"

"I think I may know where Oluwatoni is. It didn't occur to me until now. I knew I was trying to remember something else back there at the toy shop. The CCC statue. She'd slept there once. She said it made her feel safe. I only had to look for her for two minutes. There she was, lying at the statue's feet."

"Then let's go."

Kemi clasped his hand on the steering wheel.

"It's almost like our only chance, Tunde. I can't promise she'll be there."

"Are you doubting now, hon?"

And he drove off.

They neared the curve and swerved into the next road. They were stopped by the policeman who was ranting about them taking the wrong lane. Kemi flashed the picture before his eyes.

"Hey, I've seen that little girl tonight. I didn't get to know where she turned. Some nasty teenager distracted me. She was gone before I came back."

"Which way did she go?"

"I can't say. That way." He pointed right. Kemi felt her heart lighten. It was the CCC direction. The car started to move.

The policeman shouted after them. "Good luck finding your kid." Just then he sighted the runaway teenager. Raising his baton, he gave a chase.

The car was nearing the place. Kemi thought she saw a kid who looked like Oluwatoni. The car stopped and pulled over. She alighted and hurried towards the kid. She made to turn her but the mother emerged from a store.

"Who are you?" The mother flared.

"Sorry. So sorry," Kemi muttered.

"Sorry," Tunde was saying too. "We're just looking for our child."

"Well, this isn't your child." The woman said.

"We know." The couple walked away.

15

Oluwatoni could almost feel the cold eating into her. She snuggled closer to the statue, ignoring the adults that were standing few feet away, hands clasped and kneeling in prayer.

Mummy would come.

She had prayed to Jesus and she knew He had heard her. In fact, when that old woman had come to give her the small cloth to cover herself, she had thought Jesus had sent His angel to comfort her.

Mummy had made her believe in Jesus and angels. But Mummy no longer believed in Jesus. Mummy said she would leave Daddy. She had heard her say so two days ago. It would make Jesus unhappy.

Mummy said when we do wrong, Jesus will not be happy with us. But He will love us when we're good children. And she always wanted to be a good kid. She'd confessed her sins tonight. That way Jesus will not be angry with her.

She'd remembered all her lies tonight, how she'd been angry at Biola and had pushed him away. She'd prayed for Jesus to forgive the muffin man. Then she'd gone to sleep. Her legs were cold still and then she'd awoken again.

She'd turned her face away, wanting to cry. She couldn't. Wouldn't. She was Jesus' baby. She was a big girl also. Biola would be happy she didn't cry. She would see Biola again when Mummy found her.

She felt the tug.

It was light at first. Then forced. She turned. She nudged her eyes with the back of her palm. Of course, she was seeing right. Jesus had answered her prayer.

Mummy had come.

"Mummy." She muttered tiredly and threw herself into her waiting arms.

"Oh God. Oh, God. My baby. My baby. Are you okay? Are you hurt? Is there anything?" Kemi was hurriedly looking her over. People were watching, gawking. Tunde was holding the two close.

"Mummy, will you still leave daddy?" Oluwatoni asked.

Kemi looked at Tunde. The answer was in his eyes. "I doubt so, sweetheart." She'd never felt she loved him this much.

ABOUT THE AUTHOR

Busayo Lawrence is a writer, poet, copywriter, email copywriter, and a whole bunch of stuff he doesn't love to talk about. He is equally a serial entrepreneur. He helps writers become authors and authors sell more books. To find more products from the author, visit www.busayolawrence.com

Write to us or reach us:

Website: www.busayolawrence.com

Email: support@busayolawrence.com